Smart Move,
MAZU

CANDLEWICK
ENTERTAINMENT

This book is based on the episode "Think Quick" from the television series *Gigantosaurus*™.
The TV series *Gigantosaurus*™ is created and produced by Cyber Group Studios
and based on original characters created by Jonny Duddle.

First U.S. edition 2020
First published by Templar Books, an imprint of Bonnier Books UK 2020

Library of Congress Catalog Card Number pending
ISBN 978-1-5362-1407-9

20 21 22 23 24 25 TWP 10 9 8 7 6 5 4 3 2 1

Printed in Johor Bahru, Malaysia

This book was typeset in Kosmik BoldOne and Kosmik PlainTwo.
The illustrations were created digitally.

Candlewick Entertainment
an imprint of
Candlewick Press
99 Dover Street
Somerville, Massachusetts 02144

visit us at www.candlewick.com

Mazu is always coming up with
new inventions! She has hidden
ten of these spyglasses inside this book.

Can you find them all?

This story is all about **MAZU**, the awesome ankylosaurus. Mazu is the cleverest little dino in Cretacea, but there's one problem she can't seem to solve — how to run as fast as her friends! When they're all chased by the mighty Gigantosaurus, will Mazu be able to outrun the most fearsome dinosaur around?

The dinosaurs were playing a game of bone ball in the savanna. The teams were tied and it was Mazu's turn to bat.

"Get ready, Mazu. Here comes my triple flip pitch!" shouted Trey. The ball came speeding toward her, and she swung the bat as hard as she could. THWACK!

You can do it, Mazu!

Mazu ran as fast as her legs would carry her. But before she could even reach the first stone base, the other team got the ball.

"YOU'RE OUT!" they yelled. "We win!"

"It's my fault we lost," Mazu said sadly. She knew it was only a game, but she hated letting her friends down. As she spoke, there was a strong gust of wind.

"Look, the BIG WINDS are coming!" Tiny said excitedly.

The dinos in Cretacea looked forward to this day all year long. It was the only time they got to eat the delicious giant walnuts that grew in the tallest trees.

Rocky took out one of his Gigantosaurus cards to show his friends. "Usually it's only Giganto who gets the giant walnuts," he said. "But when the BIG WINDS knock them out of the trees, they're fair game . . . if you can run fast enough!"

Giganto DEFINITELY doesn't like to share!

"That's why I never get any," Mazu sighed.
"I'm just NOT fast enough."

Mazu went to sit in her favorite thinking spot on top of the den. Her dragonfly friend fluttered down to try to cheer her up.

"It's no use," Mazu said, looking at her short legs. "Ankylosauruses just aren't built for speed!"

Back on the ground, Mazu's friends were still playing bone ball. She watched Iggy bounce across the savanna and snatch the ball in mid-air.

"I wish I could run as fast as Iggy," Mazu said. "His legs are like springs!"

She looked around and spotted a coiled-up vine hanging from a tree. It looked just like a spring! Her mind started whirring. . . .

Soon enough, Mazu was standing proudly on top of a brand new invention — a pair of vine-spring shoes! She took a couple of steps forward.

"It's working. Look how fast I'm going!" she cried as she bounced along.

But as she picked up speed, Mazu began to leap more wildly. Her springy shoes were almost TOO springy.

How do I stooooop?

Suddenly, Mazu lost control and landed in a nearby tree with a THUMP!
"I guess springy legs won't work for me," she groaned.

Then the ground SHOOK so hard that Mazu tumbled out of the branches.
It was Giganto striding across the savanna.

"He's so fast," Mazu said. "If I had long legs like Giganto, I could REALLY move!"
Her mind started whirring again. . . .

It wasn't long before Mazu was wobbling over to Rocky, Bill, and Tiny in Giganto-sized steps. They stopped playing to admire her latest invention — a pair of stilts!

"Look how tall they make you!" said Bill. "I bet you can run just as fast as the rest of us now!"

"I bet I can too," replied Mazu proudly. "Just watch me!"

Those are really cool, Mazu!

But as Mazu tried to take another step forward, she lost her balance and tumbled to the ground. "I'll NEVER be fast!" she wailed.

The others couldn't understand why being speedy was so important to Mazu. She was good at plenty of other things — like thinking of incredible ideas! They decided to give her their own tips for running quickly.

Let's work with the legs you have!

First up was Rocky. "When I run, I tell myself
that I'm fast as a raptor," he said, striking a pose.

Then Tiny chipped in. "I pretend I'm light as a feather
and graceful as a springtime blossom."

"I just pretend that Giganto's after me," Bill admitted.

Now Mazu felt much more hopeful about getting a giant walnut. "I'm going to be one speedy ankylosaurus when the winds come!" she said.

And just then, the BIG WINDS started to blow. Across Cretacea, dinosaurs stopped and looked up at the sky. It was WALNUT TIME!

Let's go get some walnuts!

The four friends started running toward the tall trees, but Mazu quickly fell behind the others. They stopped to wait for her.

"We're not going without you, Mazu!" said Tiny.

"But we've been waiting for this day all year," said Mazu. "It's OK! Run ahead!"

Mazu kept on running,
remembering her friends'
advice. She tried to run as fast
as a raptor, like Rocky said.
But it was no good — even a
passing prehistoric bug could
outrun her!

Next, Mazu thought
of Tiny. She tried to be
graceful like a springtime
blossom, but immediately
tripped over a rock and
went flying into a bush.

Now there was only Bill's advice left to try.

"I guess I could try pretending Giganto is behind me," Mazu said.

But she didn't need to pretend. At that moment, the ground under her feet began to shake. She turned to see the huge green dinosaur STOMPING toward her. It was time to RUN!

AAAARRRGHH!

Rocky, Tiny, and Bill had just arrived at the giant walnut trees when they saw Mazu puffing toward them. It was the fastest they had ever seen her run!

"GIGANTO IS COMING!" shouted Mazu.

"Mazu — you took my advice!" said Bill cheerily. He thought Mazu was just pretending, but then he noticed that the ground was trembling. . . .

GIGANTOSAURUS!

"OH! Giganto's REALLY coming!" Bill cried.

The little dinos each grabbed a walnut and started running.

"This time, we're not leaving you behind, Mazu," Tiny said. "We stick together, no matter what!"

The little dinos were trying their best, but Giganto was gaining on them!

"I was hoping these big walnut leaves would hide us!" wailed Bill.

Mazu looked up at the leaves and spotted her dragonfly friend drifting along on the wind. This gave her an idea. . . .

"Everybody, hold up your walnut as HIGH as you can!" she shouted.

WHOOOAAA!

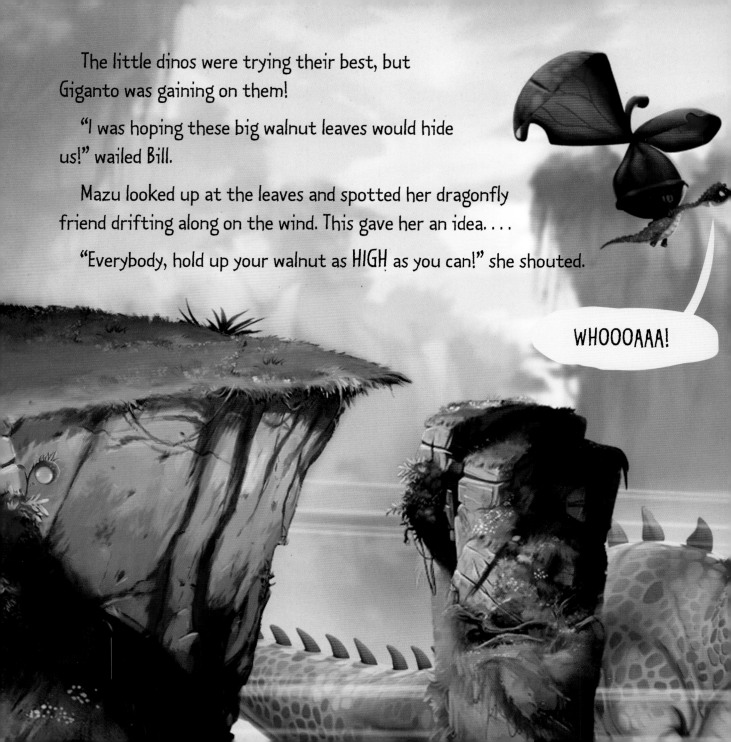

All four dinosaurs lifted their walnuts above their
heads. The wind caught the walnut leaves and lifted
them up off the ground. They were flying!

The wind swept them high above the jungle. Even
Giganto couldn't reach them there!

Mazu looked down and spotted the entrance to the Cave of Shrieks below. The little dinos used the walnut leaves like parachutes and floated gently down to the cave to hide.

"What a smart idea!" Tiny said. "You might not RUN quickly, but you sure do THINK quickly, Mazu!"

Mazu realized her friends were right. It didn't matter if she was fast on her feet!

"THIS is where I'm fast!" she said, tapping her head.

They were interrupted by a growling sound outside. GIGANTO had followed them to the cave!

Mazu realized that the big dino hadn't been chasing THEM. He wanted a walnut—just like they did! There were plenty to go around, so Mazu picked one up and rolled it outside.

"If only we had a nutcracker like that!" said Rocky, in awe of Giganto's giant jaw.

"Maybe we do!" said Mazu, and used her spiky tail to WHACK a walnut open.

The little dinosaurs cheered and gathered around to eat.
NOW it was nut time!